P9-EFI-837

Sun and Moon

LINDSEY YANKEY

Published in 2015 by Simply Read Books

www.simplyreadbooks.com

Library and Archives Canada Cataloguing in Publication
Yankey, Lindsey, author, illustrator
Sun and Moon / written and illustrated by Lindsey Yankey.
ISBN 978-1-927018-60-6 (bound)

I. Title.
PZ7.Y2Su 2015 j813'.6 C2014-905982-5
We gratefully acknowledge for their financial support of our publishing program the Canada Council for the Arts, the BC Arts Council, and the Government of Canada through the Canada Book Fund (CBF).

Manufactured in Malaysia
Book design by Robin Mitchell Cranfield for hundreds & thousands

10 9 8 7 6 5 4 3 2 1

— for E and M

"Just for one day," begged the moon.

That was all he wanted. After a lifetime in darkness, Moon wished to spend just one day as the sun.

At night, with everyone asleep,
his world was often boring
and lonely.

Moon imagined Sun
saw beautiful sights like
flowers blooming,

children playing,

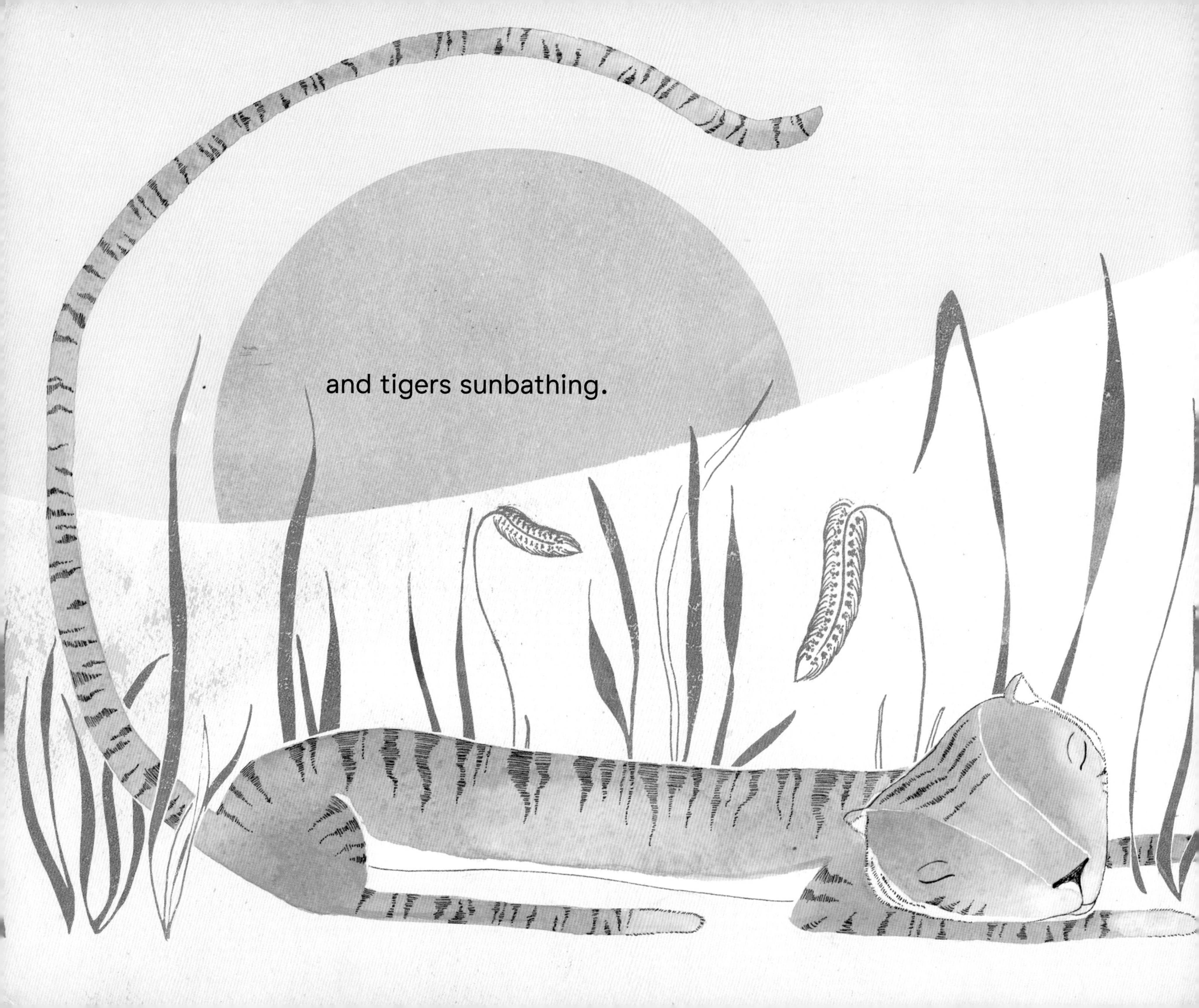

and tigers sunbathing.

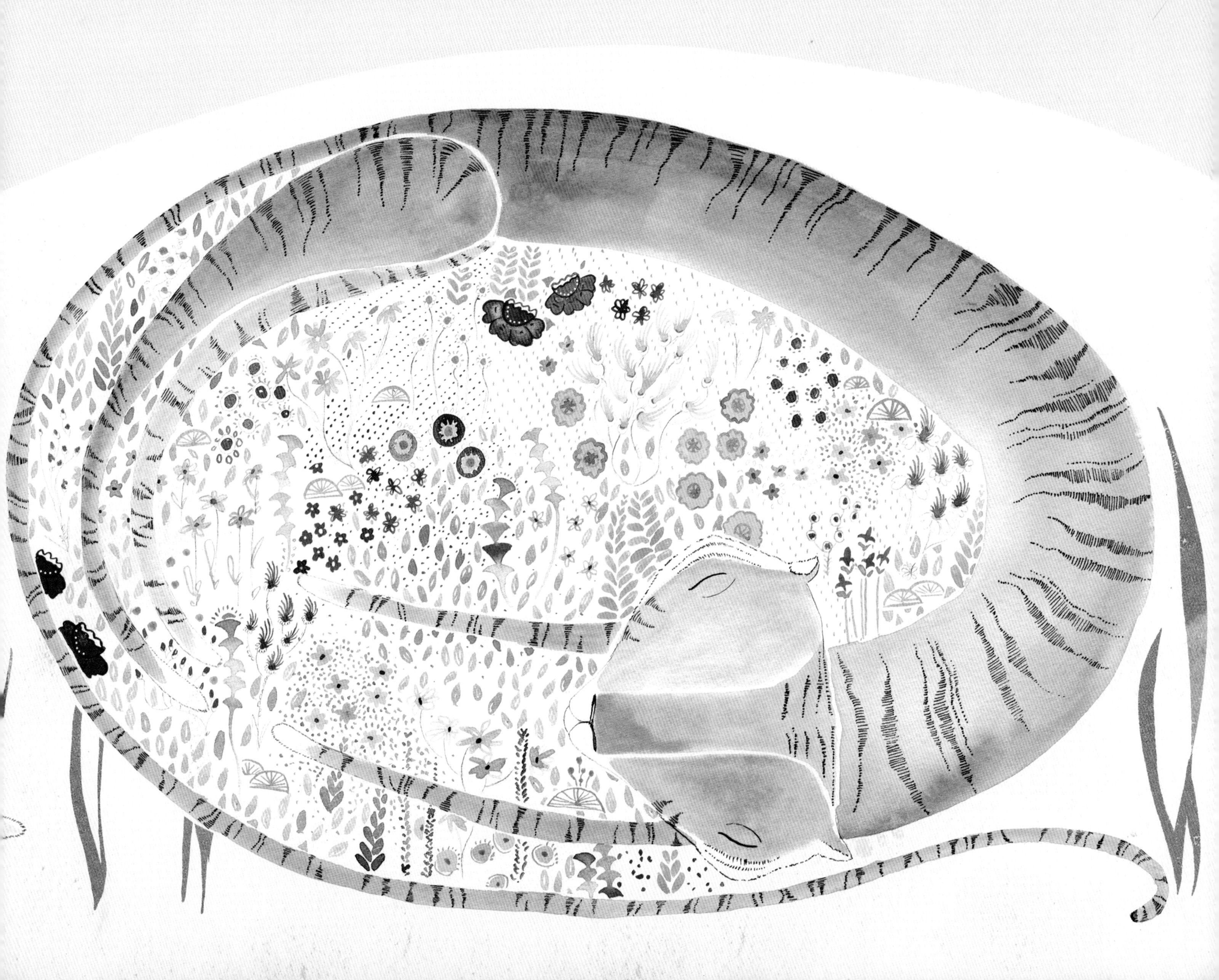

"I will only trade my day for your night if you meet two conditions," Sun told Moon. "First, if we trade, it will last forever, not just for one day.

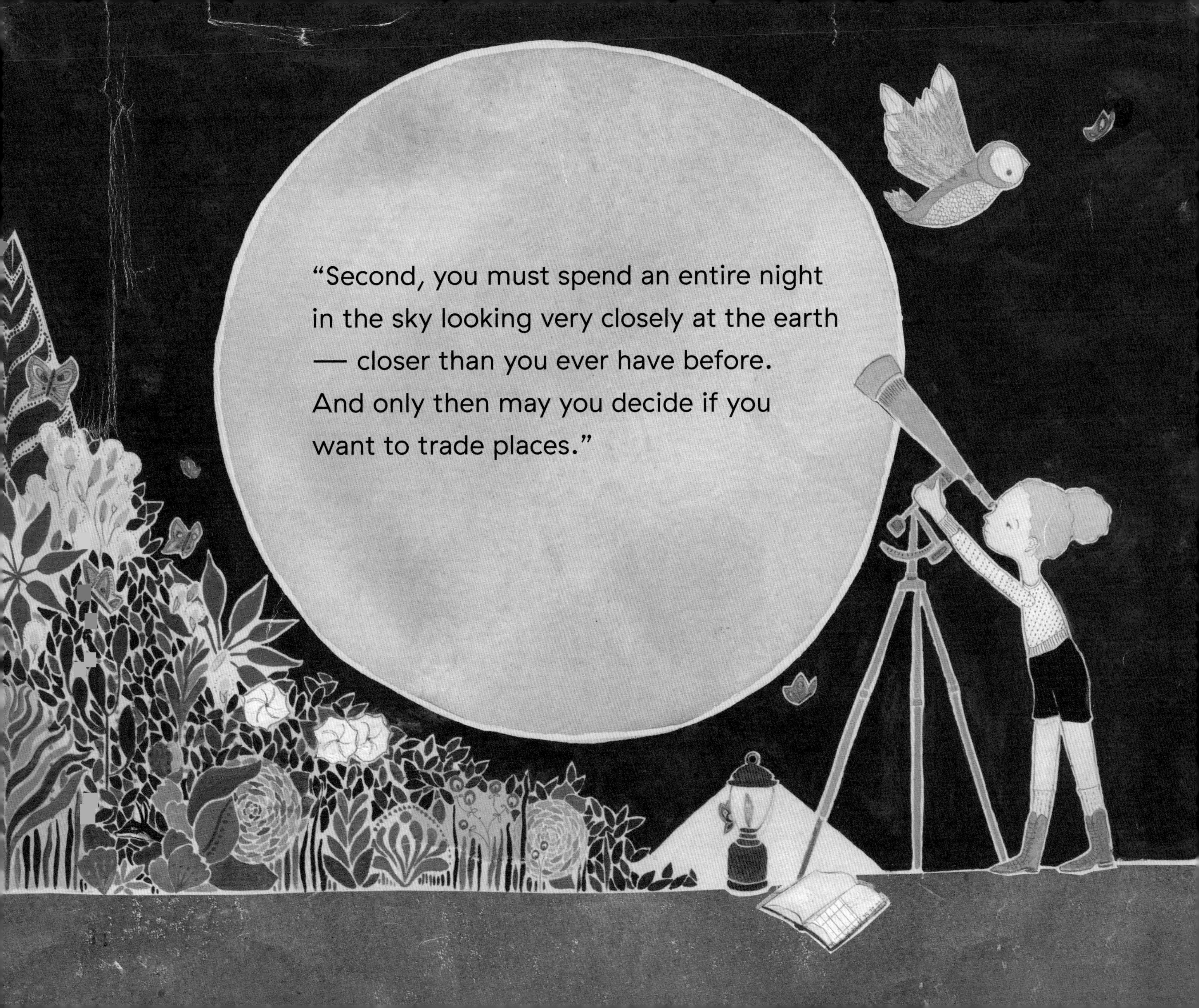

"Second, you must spend an entire night in the sky looking very closely at the earth — closer than you ever have before. And only then may you decide if you want to trade places."

Moon was thrilled! “I promise to look closer than ever before,” he told Sun.

Moon hurried to his place in the night sky. As he rose on the horizon he peered through the darkness, expecting to see nothing more than a sleepy world.

Instead, he saw the vibrant life of a nighttime carnival...

and foxes waking,

eager to hunt.

He saw the colorful lights of a city below. And through a window...

he saw children dreaming.

As the night went on,
he saw the flowers of a
baobab tree blossom.

He watched curiously as a family of raccoons set off through a forest.

He wondered where they were going and what they were up to.

Just when he thought the world
would finally fall asleep, a lamplighter
lit one more street lamp.

To Moon's amazement,
fireworks boomed
and thundered
across the sky.

Their bright colors
reminded him of
the wildflowers
in his daydreams.

Across a quiet field he saw fireflies softly glowing as they drifted closer to him and the stars. He hadn't paid much attention to the stars before, but now they were all around him, so near he could even hear them smile.

"Just for one day," he had begged. That was all he had wanted. But now, Moon wished for nothing more than to spend the rest of his nights enjoying the exciting and wonderful things that came to life in his moonlight.

At last, Sun greeted Moon and asked, “So, do you still want to trade places with me?”

“Oh no,” said Moon. “I don’t want to trade my night for anything — not even for a day.”